Help, my kid turned vegan!

A Practical Guide for Parents on How to Pretend You're Listening

MARCUS MARTIN

Copyright © 2019 Marcus Martin
All rights reserved.
www.marcusmartinauthor.com/comedy

CONTENTS

So, you're newly be-Veaged 2

Orientation Test 6

Useful Phrases 8

Regret 10

How to escape judgement 11

Role Play Exercise: Birthday Meal 16

How to spot a vegan 18

How to Win Common Arguments 22

Defending your diet 26

Wardrobe Wars 28

Shutting them up 30

Alternatives to their Alternative Facts 31

Case Study: The Langard Family 35

Vegan Parlor Games 40

Anatomy of a Vegan Brain 43

Vegan Star Signs 44

Diagnosing Your Adult Vegan Child 50

Traps 54

Summary of Learnings 56

Ha. You thought it was difficult when I was **vegetarian**.

So, you're newly ~~bereaved~~ be-Veaged

Welcome, dear parent. Veganism, hey? You always thought it was something that happened to *other* people's kids.

Shame is common among newly be-veaged parents.

Dad, I have to tell you something... I'm vegan.

Wonderful news. I'll pack your bags.

Don't blame yourself. Blame that damned school. Why would they teach them science then forget to tell kids how to ignore it? It's irresponsible.

Your child loved your cherry pie growing up — yet now they're looking at the butter pastry like it's radioactive.

They're probably showing you preachy YouTube clips, or using the phrases 'soy protein' and 'plant based' a lot.

"WHAT DO VEGANS EVEN EAT? AIR? HOW WOULD YOU COOK THAT?"
– EVA, A RECENTLY BE-VEAGED MOTHER OF TWO

Are you feeling like you're suddenly public enemy number 1? Didn't climb aboard the vegan express quick enough for the woke tyrant in your life?

THE WOKE TRAIN STOPS FOR NOBODY

HELP HAS ARRIVED.

This pioneering book will equip you with the facts and put-downs vegans wish you didn't know.

You get to have egg on your plate, while they get egg on their face. It's the second last place they want egg.

Orientation

Answer True or False for

1	Vegans have superior long-sight vision, because they're used to looking down at people from their high, high horses
2	Vegans don't eat eggs because secretly they lay them
3	The world land speed record for taking offence is held by a vegan who got irritated by the thought of a friend's party that didn't cater for her star sign
4	Vegans were deployed as geese in WWII to confuse Hitler

Test

the following statements:

5	Vegans have a longer life expectancy than omnivores, but waste it by spending all their time whining
6	Vegans are actually descended from a separate branch of humans called Woko sapiens
7	If you stretched all the vegans on earth out in a line, they'd reach to the moon and back twice before someone called the police

Find the answers in your heart. If you get stuck, close your eyes and rub a pack of bacon to summon your Fairy Meatmother. She's got your back. Or at least, she's got *someone's* back. Naughty Meatmother, what's she like!

Useful Phrases

Escape all those judgey looks and snide remarks when you meet your kids' friends. Use these common phrases to pass as a vegan.

Let's get out of here and go milk some nuts

I THINK VEGAN CHEESE IS BETTER THAN REGULAR CHEESE, IT JUST TASTES SO AUTHENTIC

Kale for president

I RECENTLY TORE UP ALL THE GRASS ON MY LAWN SO I COULD GROW SAND INSTEAD

OMG THAT IS SOOOO PLANT BASED

I'm trying to cut down at work so I can spend more time at the soup kitchen (their selection is fantastic)

HASHTAG 'ONIONS'!

Did you see that new David Attenborough series? It sure looks like us humans are doing great things to the planet.

Regret

When your kid turns out to be vegan, it can be easy to blame yourself.

Tick everything you're feeling:

- [ ] I should never have paid for their education
- [x] It's a phase. Please God, tell me it's a phase
- [ ] I'm changing the locks
- [x] They're doing this to upset me
- [ ] Is vegan the same as gay? I can handle that so long as they eat meat

PREPARING FOR CONVERSATION WITH A VEGAN

How to escape judgement

Some vegans can be very persistent. Once they've smelled last night's lamb tagine on your sweater, it can be hard to shake them off. Here are a number of tactics you can use, with illustrative examples.

New email from Tery: "Veganism is kindness"

Deleted.

REMIND THEM YOU'RE A GOOD PERSON

I always walk to my Uber, and only fly sixteen times a year.

SOUND WORDLY

I think we should be focusing our energies on curing cancer, not eating carrots.

BLACKMAIL THEM

Didn't you eat a cracker last week that was processed in a factory that handles bees which may contain milk?

USE THE SLIPPERY SLOPE ARGUMENT

If we stop eating animals, it's only a matter of time before they say plants have feelings too. What would I eat then, plastic bags? Pff, please. I'm not a turtle.

BEAT THEM AT THEIR OWN GAME

If you don't eat meat, I'll double my meat intake. I will offset your veganism.

ARTIST'S DEPICTION OF A VEGAN MIND GOING THROUGH MEAT WITHDRAWAL

Everything's fine.
I've barely noticed the adjustment.

SCIENTIFIC EVIDENCE THAT VEGANISM IS BAD

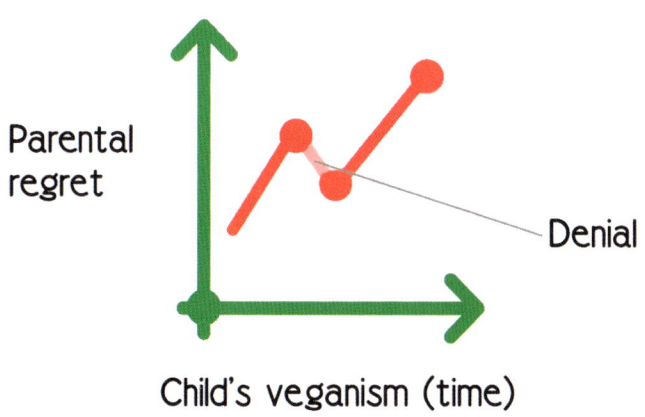

Role Play Exercise: Birthday Meal

Your glowing vegan kid says to you:

"I WANT TO EAT AT THIS NEW VEGAN RESTAURANT TONIGHT, TO HAVE A CRUELTY-FREE BIRTHDAY"

Do you say:

    a. Enjoy the loneliest birthday in the history of man

    b. I'll show *you* cruelty....

    c. I'd rather *eat* an ass than listen to one

Top tip: Remember, they may have values, but you've got a steady income and a house. Joke's on them.

If you don't have these things, no worries, you've still got age on your side. Think back to a time when your kid was incontinent. Remind them of it cruelly and often until they stop visiting.

Look nana, I made this cake - it's delicious & 100% plant based

You disgust me.

How to spot a vegan

Complexion

Something's probably wrong. Look at their face. Did it always look like that? I bet it didn't.

Posture

Vegans love to stand. It reminds them they hold the high ground. However, you'll often find them sitting down too. This can be for two reasons:

a. Their weak vegan legs can't hack it in the upright world
b. It gon' rain

Hiding in a group

Typical bloody herbivores. They love nothing more than a good herd. Most vegan herds exist online, where they can share videos of ponies crying and conspiracy theories about meat eaters. Sometimes vegan herds will migrate to a watering hole, where they can find plant-based milks. Accompany them, wait for them to order, then point to the stylish filament bulbs and ask them what the energy efficiency rating is. It's probably way lower than a pig's.

Being Skinny

Remember how they used to look like Lance Armstrong? (Before he was disgraced). Now they probably look like Lance Armstrong (since he's been disgraced).

Standing out

Vegans also like to use petulance. It helps them to alienate everyone within a 10 mile radius. This leaves them exposed, so their virtue can be signaled from a distance.

TOP TIP:

If you're unsure whether or not someone's vegan, ask them for directions to the nearest bus stop. It'll come up.

How to Win Common Arguments

Vegans love to argue. Don't let their whiny ways wear you down. Use these comebacks to steal their eco-thunder. All responses below have been field-tested on living vegans, with 100% results.

 ANIMALS ARE SENTIENT.

 Really? Then how come they've never predicted the lottery?

 VEGANISM IS BETTER FOR THE ENVIRONMENT.

 I think it's time you presented some hard evidence that this 'environment' you speak of even exists.

 HAVE YOU THOUGHT ABOUT REDUCING YOUR MEAT INTAKE?

 Yes. I also thought about reducing your allowance. Which should I do first?

DEVELOPED NATIONS LIKE US HAVE TO LEAD THE WAY ON THIS.

 Er, we gave the world Netflix. I think we've done our bit.

 I GET ALL MY ESSENTIAL AMINO ACIDS FROM PLANTS.

 You can't eat acid, dummy. What you need is protein.

 THE EGG INDUSTRY GETS RID OF MALE CHICKS AT BIRTH. WOULD YOU HAVE GOT RID OF ME IF I WAS A BOY?

 No. I'd have got a factory to do it.

NOTHING SAYS "NATURAL" LIKE PILLS OF PULVERIZED SEAWEED

OOH, THE CANTEEN'S GOT VENISON BURGERS

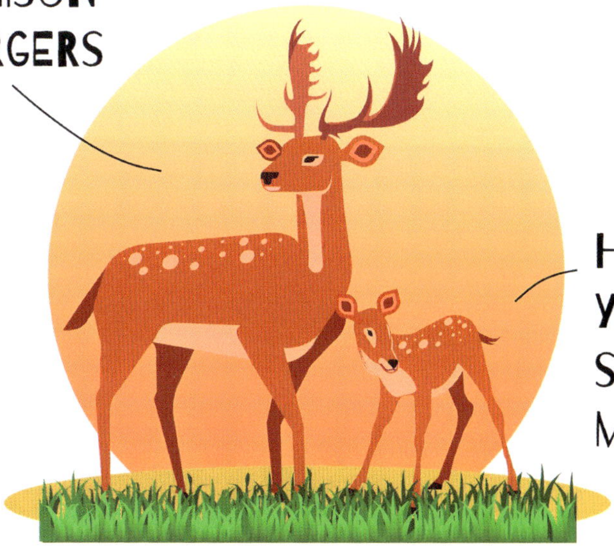

HAVE YOU SEEN MOM?

Defending your diet

Don't let a vegan catch you out over dinner. Swat up on these common accusations, and memorize the responses.

WHAT IF I WORE *YOUR* FAMILY OUT TO DINNER, THEN ATE YOUR COUSINS?

 I don't think you'd be allowed back in the restaurant

 FREE RANGE HENS AREN'T FREE AT ALL

 Agreed – that's why I buy caged eggs

 DO YOU EVEN KNOW HOW THE DAIRY INDUSTRY WORKS?

 Yes. Where else do you think we got the idea of adopting you?

 CHICKENS ARE SUPPOSED TO LIVE IN TREES

 If we filled our trees with chickens, they'd eat all the leaves and the forest would die. Is that what you want?

Wardrobe Wars

It's not just about food. These crazy vegans object to people doing pretty much anything with animals – whether it's eating their flesh, wearing their skin, or rubbing makeup into their eyes. They call it 'consistency'. The rest of us call it a pain in the ass.

I CAN'T WAIT TO TELL YOU HOW WRONG YOU ARE

Here's how to get through a fashion fight with a vegan

 HOW CAN YOU WEAR THAT BELT WHEN IT'S MADE OF SUFFERING?

 IT'S MADE OF SUEDE, DUMBASS.

 DID YOU KNOW FUR IS REMOVED WHILE THE ANIMAL'S STILL ALIVE?

 NO, BECAUSE I WASN'T THERE. CLEARLY YOU WERE THOUGH, YOU SICK PERVERT.

 THERE ARE LOADS OF COMFORTABLE, DURABLE, ECO-FRIENDLY TEXTILES AVAILABLE THESE DAYS.

 YOU KNOW WHAT ELSE IS AVAILABLE? SILENCE.

Shutting them up

It can be hard getting your point across to a vegan, no matter how unreasonable you are.

Here are the latest police guidelines on negotiating with those difficult plant-eating mouth bags.

Try reasoning with them:
 Shut up... Please.

Try to understand their demands:
 I hear what you're saying, I'm just ignoring it, OK?

Offer a compromise:
 I'll buy you an oat-milk Frappuccino if you stop speaking for five minutes.

Disarm them:
 Put. The. Kale. Down.

Alternatives to their Alternative Facts

Vegans think they know it all. But here's a secret... they don't! Catch them out in conversation with these handy facts of your own.

CARBON FACT
Lots of vegan food is imported by sea, which generates carbon, unlike meat which reaches my mouth via a fork.

PAIN FACT
Animals can't feel pain – the only ones that do are donkeys, who look sad all the time. That's why I don't eat donkey.

ISLAND FACT
What about people who live in islands and can only grow fish? Fish don't grow on trees, dummy. That's money.

FOREST FACT
How are we going to get rid of the rainforests if we stop eating beef?

FARMING FACT
Industrial soy bean farming can cause a monoculture which is bad. It's no different to farming maize or wheat, other than I recently learned the word 'monoculture'.

BIBLIOGRAPHY
Gut instinct.

UH, WE'RE NOT A MONOCULTURE... THERE'S TWO OF US.

This little piggy went wee wee wee wee all the way to an animal welfare rally

Case Study: The Langard Family

Pete's daughters were both diagnosed with veganism less than 12 months ago. This is his story.

The interviewer's text is in orange.
For anonymity, Pete asked that we print his words in gray.

Describe a typical day in your household.

I get up, fry some eggs, my kids call me a Nazi, then I go to work. For the record, I'm not a Nazi. I just like French toast.

Why would your kids make that comparison?

They say I am one in the chicken world.

Wait, you're saying there's a separate world belonging to chickens, and a fascist state has taken power? Should we send help?

I think it's a metaphor. I'm not really into politics. Like I said, I just like breakfast.

Home sounds stressful. Is work a safe place for you?

There are some vegans there. They put a sign up showing the carbon footprint of the different milk options by the coffee machine, and added smiley faces.

That doesn't sound too bad?

They used Comic Sans.

Patronizing jerks. Fire them all.

Oh, I don't have that kind of power — I'm middle management.

What's it like coming home at night?

Depends on the traffic.

I mean, do you dread seeing your vegan kids?

Frankly, each time I get back I'm amazed they're still alive. I ask them what they ate, and they're like 'plant stuff', then smile like that freakin' milk sign.

They get by all day eating plants? What's even in that?

I dunno. Grass?

Pff, right. So when you get home, what's meal time like?

It's a real battle. They'll try and trick me with all these alternatives, which taste fine, but I'm still feeling like, 'where's my meat?'

Is getting meat important to you?

It's who I am.

You're meat?

I guess… I mean, I don't wanna be eaten.

That answers my next question. Moving on, what's your biggest regret about having vegan children?

Manners. It's like they gave up meat, and gave up basic conversational politeness with it. I don't actually care what they eat, so long as they're healthy. I just want them to remember that they were brought up with manners. And meat.

How are you all coping?

I can't say or do anything right without offending them.

What have you said or done?

I told them meat was great and ordered loads of it.

How did they take it?

They waited until I'd finished eating, then showed me how sausage is made.

Barbarians.

I keep asking myself 'what did I do wrong?' Then I remember I don't need to, because they tell me every second of every day.

Do you think your daughters' veganism is just a phase?

I wish. No, they're in it for the long haul.

What makes you think that?

They're both happy, healthy, and annoyingly well-informed. What am I supposed to do?

Have you tried changing the WiFi password?

I don't know how to do that.

What about the health angle – have you challenged them on that?

Yeah, they say they're getting everything they need from plants, then show me a bunch of websites. I think it's all bull. I don't know any living things that can survive off plants alone.

THERE'S NO EASY WAY TO TELL YOU THIS, SON...
WE LIVE REALLY LONG, REMEMBER REALLY WELL,
AND BRING BALANCE AND HARMONY TO OUR ECOSYSTEM

GASP - WE'RE MONSTERS!

Vegan Parlor Games

THE RICE IS RIGHT

Courtroom gameshow. Take turns playing Judge Jadey – a sassy bowl of steaming basmati who isn't afraid to say it how it is. If a contestant is found guilty of liking butter, other players get to pelt them with grains of the white stuff.

WHOSE PINE IS IT ANYWAY?

Each of you tries a handful of different seeds, blindfolded. The winner is the first to correctly identify the hidden pine nut. Everyone's a winner though, with a healthy source of omega 3, 6, and 9.

VEAL OR NO VEAL

Half of you play industrially-reared fawns. You're kept in a cage and partially sedated, while the other contestants fatten you up for market. At the end of the game you get fed into a mincer. It's a family favorite.

WE WIN AGAIN!

FOR THE RECORD, I VOTED WE PLAY SCRABBLE

NAME THAT SHROOM

Players take turns rubbing different varieties of wild fungi in each other's ears. The winner is the person who can hear the correct answer. They're crowned the 'mushroom whisperer'.

THE CRYSTAL MAIZE

Each team is equipped with a corn on the cob, an R.V, and season 1 of Breaking Bad. They have one week to produce a highly addictive psychoactive substance and sell it to the neighbor's kids, before mom gets home.

MORMON VEGAN OF THE YEAR 1999

Anatomy of a Vegan Brain

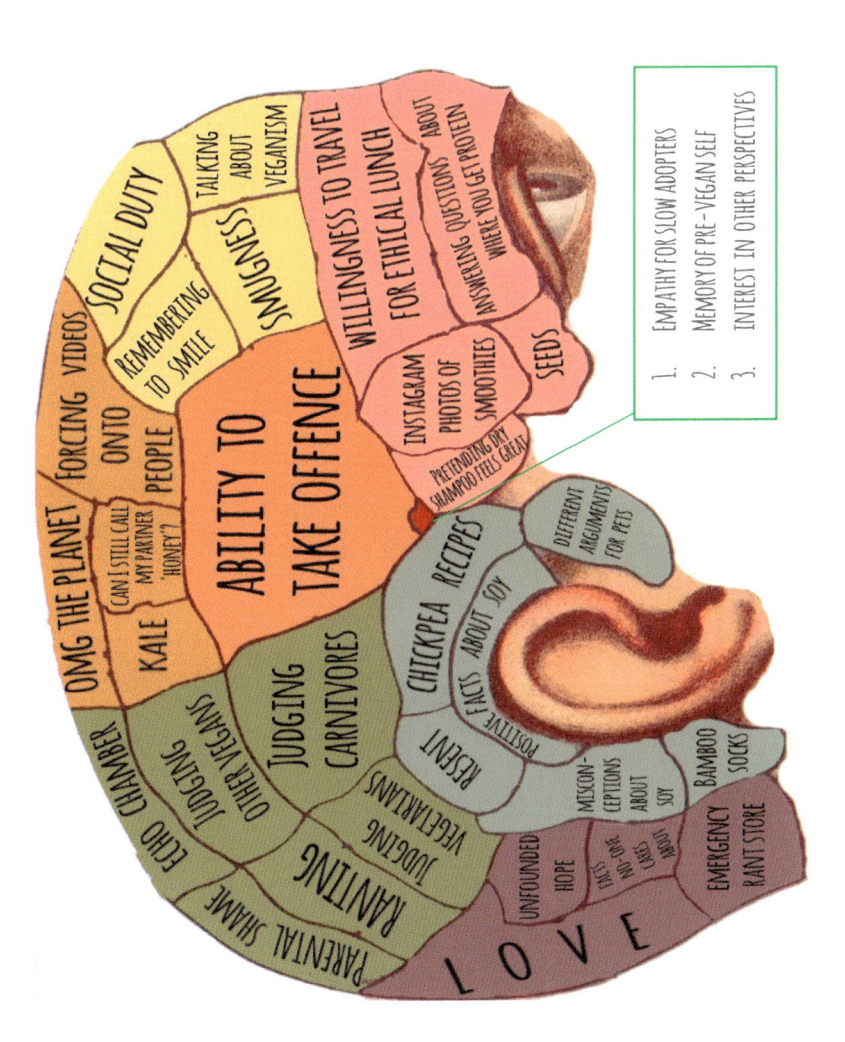

- SOCIAL DUTY
- TALKING ABOUT VEGANISM
- FORCING VIDEOS ONTO PEOPLE
- REMEMBERING TO SMILE
- SMUGNESS
- WILLINGNESS TO TRAVEL FOR ETHICAL LUNCH
- ANSWERING QUESTIONS ABOUT WHERE YOU GET PROTEIN
- INSTAGRAM PHOTOS OF SMOOTHIES
- SEEDS
- PRETENDING DRY SHAMPOO FEELS GREAT
- OMG THE PLANET
- KALE
- CAN I STILL CALL MY PARTNER 'HONEY'?
- ABILITY TO TAKE OFFENCE
- DIFFERENT ARGUMENTS FOR PETS
- CHICKPEA RECIPES
- POSITIVE FACTS ABOUT SOY
- ECHO CHAMBER
- JUDGING OTHER VEGANS
- JUDGING CARNIVORES
- JUDGING VEGETARIANS
- RESENT MISCONCEPTIONS ABOUT SOY
- BAMBOO SOCKS
- PARENTAL SHAME
- RANTING
- UNFOUNDED HOPE
- FACTS NO-ONE CARES ABOUT
- EMERGENCY RANT STORE
- LOVE

1. EMPATHY FOR SLOW ADOPTERS
2. MEMORY OF PRE-VEGAN SELF
3. INTEREST IN OTHER PERSPECTIVES

Vegan Star Signs

Don't blame your loved one,
blame destiny

Aries

Highly skilled at rolling their eyes. Prone to flatulence owing to excessive fructose in their diet.

Taurus

Has a tendency to 'fact check' people's claims during a conversation. Beware – they may use underhand tactics like credible sources and reasoned debate. Avoid.

Gemini

Loves to keep pulses and dried fruit in glass jars and label them in chalk pen. Disgustingly cute. Next time you're round, find the pen, and replace the word 'flour' with an obscenity of your choosing.

Cancer

Crabby by name, crabby by nature. Think twice before becoming romantically involved..

Leo

Named after the Greek god 'Mufassa'. When a vegan Leo is born, the parent holds their child up over a rock and says "One day, all of this will be alfalfa." The child usually defecates during the ceremony.

Virgo

Their weakness is using almond milk, even though they know it's more water intensive than soya milk. Remind them of this often. Then roll your eyes like an Aries to confuse them.

Libra

These vegans were pre-emptively banned by financial regulators in several countries. They sold the family cow to buy a bunch of magic beans, and shares in the Impossible Food Company.

Scorpio

I saw a BuzzFeed article once that said these guys are campaigning to have small pox released back into the wild.

Sagittarius

Vegans do not acknowledge the legitimacy of Sagittarius.

Capricorn

Every time they mention veganism, you get a point. When you reach six points in a day shout Ve-gingo! You may then perform a culturally appropriative rain dance until you're asked to leave.

Aquarius

Never reveal your carnivorous ways to an Aquarius. They'll throw you under the first electric bus they see.

Pisces

Being sat next to a Pisces vegan at a dinner party is a fate worse than death. Like a pilot fish, they'll use a big smile to lure you into conversation. Then they'll pretend to listen to your views, before enjoying a nutritionally-balanced meal that they brought.

Go vegan, it's written in the stars!

Dammit Sagittarius, we're not all 50% horse

EINSTEIN'S LAW OF VEGANISM:
THE CONSERVATION OF SMUGNESS

$$V = mc^2$$

M = NO. OF DAYS WITHOUT MEAT
C = CAN'T SHUT UP ABOUT IT

NOT AGAIN

HOUSTON WE HAVE A PROBLEM...
ONE OF THE ASTRONAUTS IS VEGAN.
THEY'VE ALREADY TAKEN OFFENCE.

IT'S THE 21ST CENTURY, PEOPLE.
HOW CAN THE MOON NOT
HAVE DAIRY-FREE MILK?

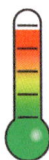

Diagnosing Your Adult Vegan Child

Where's your overgrown kidult on the vegan scale?

-1 FRAUD

They tell certain people they're vegan, but mainly to get laid.

0 CARNIVORE

Test this by feeding them a sausage. If they're still happy to chew on a reconstituted face, hoof, or buttock, you're good to go. If the packet has a smiling pig, all the better. That pig knows the deal, and it loves it (probably).

1 FLEXETARIAN

If they claim this for more than six months, it means they're full of crap and just like to sound good in conversation. Smile at them, ruffle their hair, and get yourself another beer. Careful though, if it's a new thing it might be some sort of 'gateway' ethics that could lead them to harder, more coherent ethics.

2 VEGETARIAN

OK, things are getting pesky, but don't worry – they haven't joined up all the dots yet. Keep ordering pizza and talking about how the dairy industry is actually a myth invented by the communists to push down sales of tree milk.

3 VEGAN ADJACENT

They're easing themselves in, but aren't fully committed to the cause. Slip a pamphlet about limescale into their backpack and maybe you'll scare them back to common sense.

4 REGULAR VEGAN

All is not lost – we'll get through this. Just take deep breaths, flush the toilet where you're undoubtedly reading this, and go make a strong cup of coffee.

5 PRESIDENT OF THE UNITED STATES OF VEGANISTAN

I didn't vote for this – and neither did you. Time for a re-election. Go fry up all the meat-free proteins in their house, and enjoy a delicious feast at their expense. That's called democracy – a dish best served stolen.

Remember: vegans are cunning little foxes.
They've found ways to eat healthy, balanced diets
with lower carbon footprints and zero cruelty.
*If you buy and eat all their vegan food,
they'll starve, and you'll win.*

Mom, Dad, if I tasted like bacon, you'd still love me in the normal way, right?

Turn the grill off — I said *If*.
OK you've answered my question.

Hey everyone

I watched some YouTube clips and now I'm intolerable

Traps

Vegans like to lay traps in conversations.

Common signs a trap is being laid:

- They're starting to sound unusually reasonable
- They're taking a genuine interest in your perspective
- They've offered you some vegan cookies and dammit they taste fantastic

How to beat them at their own game:

- Smile often, give them hugs, and tell them you respect their intentions
- See if you can steal their wallet during the embrace
- Using their social security number, open a fake bank account
  - Use the funds to invest heavily in soy beans
  - Stockpile soy beans
  - Sell the beans back to them at an extortionate mark-up

How to pretend you're listening:

- Part your lips slightly – this makes it look like you're about to respond to a point they're making, when really it's an opportunity to breathe through your mouth undetected
- Nod your head diagonally, like you're tracing a tear drop – to a vegan, this implies you're empathizing with their perspective, and are mulling it over. Really, you're just shaking your head

Darling, I'd love to hear more about coconut oil but I'm going into a tunnel

Summary

So, what have you learned?

- If a random vegan falls from its nest and you pick it up, its natural mother will reject it

- Vegans can be taller or shorter than you think, but either way they'll be annoying

- Vegans only rest one brain hemisphere at a time. This allows oxygen to flow through their gills, and one hand to constantly tweet about the patriarchy

- If you've got a vegan coming to dinner, don't sweat it. Just give them all the vegetable side dishes, then tell them they're looking sickly and thin

- If they offer to bring their own meal, it's a trap. They'll almost certainly need to use some of your non-vegan electricity to heat it up. Send them an invoice two weeks after the meal and make it out to 'The Leek-Licking Hypocrite'

Congratulations! You're now ready to go forth into the big woke world, and counter-patronize every vegan you meet.
Start with the vegan that bought you this book.
It's the least they deserve.

Eric says "bye, everyone."
What's a McNugget?

Get more
hilarious comedy
from Marcus Martin

Sign up at:
marcusmartinauthor.com/comedy

Follow on FB: @MarcusMartinComedy

New releases coming soon

Satirical Short Stories by Marcus Martin

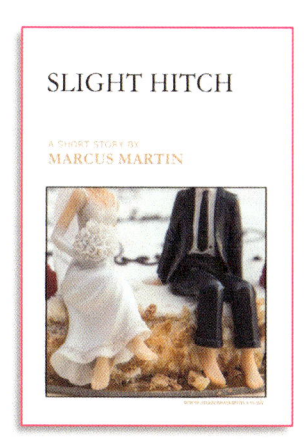

Slight Hitch

A wedding farce with a twist. Their job was to ensure the big day runs smoothly. But there's a catch. They're trapped on top of a cake, and both made of icing. And one of them has a hidden agenda...

Good Idea, Caesar!

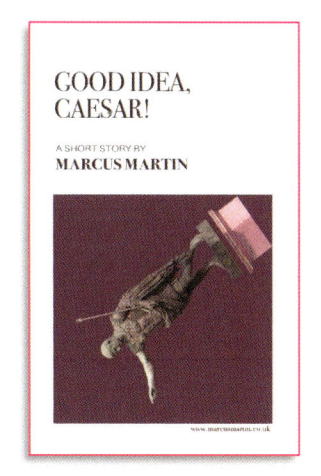

A comedy caper brimming with twists, turns, and togas. It's Rome as you've never known it. The department for "Good Ideas" has incurred Caesar's wrath. The director's gone AWOL. Can the hapless servants find her before they're fed to the lions? (Warning: adult humor)

Available now at marcusmartinauthor.com/trios

Printed in Great Britain
by Amazon